The Halloween Parade

Text and jacket art by

Rosemary Wells

Interior illustrations by

Jody Wheeler

Hyperion Books for Children

New York

Volo and the Volo colophon are trademarks of Disney Enterprises, Inc.
All rights reserved. No part of this book may be reproduced or transmitted in
any form or by any means, electronic or mechanical, including photocopying,
recording, or by any information storage and retrieval system, without written
permission from the publisher. For information address
Hyperion Books for Children, 114 Fifth Avenue,
New York, New York 10011-5690.

Printed in the United States of America

First Edition
1 3 5 7 9 10 8 6 4 2

LIBRARY OF CONGRESS CATALOGING-IN-PUBLICATION DATA
Wells, Rosemary.
The Halloween parade / Rosemary Wells.
p.   cm. — (Yoko and friends—school days/—; 3)
Summary: Yoko and Timothy aren't very frightening in their costumes that
look like food, but they can still scare Doris and Stumpy, who ride an almost-
real motorcycle in the school's Halloween parade.
ISBN 0-7868-0723-7 (hardcover)—ISBN 0-7868-1529-9 (pbk.)
[1. Halloween—Fiction. 2. Contests—Fiction. 3. Parades—Fiction.
4. Schools—Fiction.]
I. Title.
PZ7.W46843 Hal 2001
[E]—dc21   00-57260

Visit www.hyperionchildrensbooks.com

"Who is walking with you, Yoko?"

Timothy asked.

"This is Muriel," said Yoko.

"Muriel holds my hand

when we get off the bus.

I walk her to the play-school

room so that she is not afraid."

"She looks like the queen of the

bugs," said Timothy.

"Muriel is a butterfly

for Halloween," said Yoko.

"What are you going to be,

Yoko?" Timothy asked.

"A California roll," said Yoko.

"How about you?"

"I am going to be spinach," said

Timothy. "Spinach is easy to be."

"Doris and her cousin, Stumpy, are going to be Smell's Angels for Halloween," said Timothy. "I thought Doris was going to be a fairy," said Yoko.

"Not anymore. Stumpy is making her ride with him," said Timothy.

"Ride what?" asked Yoko.

"Stumpy has an almost real motorcycle. It makes a noise like a chain saw," said Timothy.

"Chain saw!" said Muriel.

"Muriel does not like chain saws," said Yoko.

Timothy whispered, "The Franks
are going to be twin Frankensteins
with real blood scars."

"Hurt!" said Muriel.

"The Franks will not really be
hurt, Muriel," said Yoko.

"They are just Franks and they
will never be Frankensteins.
I will see you later, Muriel, at the
Halloween Parade."

At two o'clock in the afternoon

Mrs. Jenkins handed out

pumpkin cookies and apple juice.

The class sang the Snack song.

"*We love our snack, snack, snack*

Won't give it back, back, back.

We love to eat, eat, eat

Down to our feet, feet, feet.

And when we're finished,

finished, finished,

We're clean and neat, neat, neat."

"Boys and girls!" said Mrs. Jenkins.

"All the classes in Hilltop School

march in the Halloween Parade,

but only one person can win

the prize."

"I'm going to win!" said Nora.

"No, me!" said Grace.

"What do we say when our
neighbor wins the prize,
boys and girls?" asked Mrs.
Jenkins.

"Congratulations to you!" shouted
the class.

"That is right," said Mrs. Jenkins.

"Now, line up, and no running!"

Everyone ran to the coatroom.

Grace was a ballerina.

Charles was a ghost.

Nora was a princess.

Fritz was a scientist.

Timothy put on a brown bag with

crepe-paper spinach stapled all over.

Yoko wrapped herself into a

California roll.

The Franks poured a bottle of fake
blood on their heads.

Doris's cousin, Stumpy,

came to the door.

"Mrs. Jenkins, may I see Doris?"

he asked. "We need to get ready

for the parade."

"Yes, Stumpy," said Mrs. Jenkins.

Doris followed Stumpy down the

hall. She didn't look happy.

"Did you see that?" asked Timothy.

"Yes. Come on!" said Yoko.

"Where to?" asked Timothy.

"To Mr. Wagweed's science room!" said Yoko.

"Why?" asked Timothy.

"I have an idea," said Yoko.

Nobody noticed that a California
roll and a bunch of spinach
sneaked down the hall.
Nobody saw them enter
the science room.
Nobody heard them open
Mr. Wagweed's secret drawer.

The Halloween Parade began

in the cafeteria.

It wound out the door

into the playground.

The fifth-graders were very fancy.

"Oh, they'll win," whined Grace.

"It's not fair. No one will look at

my pretty costume."

But the three judges

did look at Grace's costume.

"Very nice," they said.

"Keep moving, boys and girls."

Suddenly there was

a terrible noise.

It was followed by

a terrible smell of smoke.

Stumpy, dressed in black leather
with a Road Rat helmet and lots
of chains, zoomed into the
playground on his
make-believe motorcycle.

Doris rode behind him, holding

on tight.

Dust swirled. Smoke poured out.

No one could hear.

Around and around they went.

All the play-school children

ran away.

Stumpy parked under a tree.

Oil leaked from the engine.

"We're the best! We want to win!"

yelled Stumpy.

Doris held her ears.

Yoko and Timothy found Muriel

in the play-school room, hiding

under her desk.

She was too afraid of Stumpy to

come out.

"Come with us, Muriel,"

said Timothy.

"We are going to give Stumpy

the scare of the year."

Nobody heard a California roll

climb up the back side

of the oak tree.

No one noticed

a bunch of spinach follow behind.

Nobody saw a little butterfly

disappear into the branches

of the tree.

"We are going to announce

the winner, boys and girls!"

said a voice on the loudspeaker.

"We're going to win!

We're going to win!

We're going to win!" shouted

Stumpy. Doris coughed.

Suddenly, Stumpy jumped.

Off came his chains.

Off came his leather jacket and

Road Rat helmet.

Stumpy disappeared around the

back of the school.

"What happened to Stumpy?"

said Mrs. Jenkins.

Doris shrugged her shoulders, and

then she smiled.

"Look!" said Fritz.

"It's Mr. Wagweed's stuffed

tarantula. "

No one ever figured out

how the tarantula spun a web

all the way down the tree

to Stumpy's nose.

It was a mystery.

The Halloween Prize

was announced.

It went to Muriel

for her beautiful butterfly wings.

And everybody sang,

"Congratulations to you!"

Dear Parents,

When our children were young we lived in a small house, but we always made a space just for books. When their dad or I would read a story out loud, the TV was always off—radio and music, too—because it intruded.

Soon this peaceful half hour of every day became like a little island vacation. Our children are lifetime readers now with an endless curiosity for the rich world waiting between the covers of good books. It cost us nothing but time well spent and a library card.

This set of easy-to-read books is about the real nitty-gritty of elementary school. There are new friends, and bullies, too. There are germs and the "Clean Hands" song, new ways of painting pictures, learning music, telling the truth, gossiping, teasing, laughing, crying, separating from Mama, scary Halloweens, and secret valentines. The stories are all drawn from the experiences my children had in school.

It's my hope that these books will transport you and your children to a setting that's familiar, yet new. And that it will prove to be a place where you can explore the exciting new world of school together.

Rosemary Wells